Coyote Winter

Written and illustrated by
JACQUELINNE WHITE

LESTER
PUBLISHING
LIMITED

In loving memory of my sisters

Doreen White Elliott
June 30, 1922 - July 11, 1988

and

Lillian White D.C.
February 19, 1921 - June 3, 1990

who with characteristic generosity helped me to fulfill
my promise to Doreen that her story would be written.

For Carla

Canadian Cataloguing in Publication Data

White, Jacquelinne
Coyote winter
1-895555-14-0
I. Title.
PS8595.H57C6 1991   jC813'.54   C91-094402-4
PZ7.W55Co 1991

Lester Publishing Limited
56 The Esplanade
Toronto, Ontario
Canada M5E 1A7

91 92 93 94 5 4 3 2 1

Printed and bound in Hong Kong

Prologue

My sister, Doreen White Elliott, taught in a Hutterite colony in Alberta for many years. She told me this story six months before she died on July 11, 1988. She asked me to write and illustrate it in her memory.

The Hutterites originated in Germany in 1528. They were severely persecuted for their beliefs and fled to Eastern Europe, particularly to the Ukraine in Russia. They lived in Russia for 350 years but retained their German language. In the late nineteenth and beginning of the twentieth century the Hutterites were again forced to leave in order to preserve their religious freedom. Many settled in the Dakotas. In 1918 some left the United States and resettled in the prairie provinces of Canada - Alberta, Saskatchewan and Manitoba.

The Hutterites live on large farms which are owned by the colony and not by individuals. They work their farms together and eat together. They all dress very like they did in the nineteenth century. There are about 150 people in each colony and when it gets bigger another is started.

The Hutterites are a peace-loving, industrious, Christian people. Doreen loved them, especially their children. The events in this story may not have actually occurred, but the story is certainly true in spirit.

The winter that Mrs. Elliot freed the coyote was the harshest the children could remember. Week after dreary week the cold winds blew. No rippling chickadee song rang out, no saucy crows could be seen, no yipping of a coyote was heard. The animals were all hidden in hollow trees, in burrows, in tunnels deep in the ground, all covered by snow. The snow drifted higher than the windowsills. It was so dark in the middle of the day that the lights had to be kept burning. In the tiny Hutterite village on the vast prairie the homes and farm buildings seemed to draw closer to one another, as if they were trapped by the cold. The paths between the buildings became trenches with snow shovelled as high as the roofs on either side.

That winter a blizzard suddenly raged so fiercely that people could not find their way in the whirling snow. Startled by the wild rush of the storm the children gathered in fear at the windows of the schoolhouse. Soon the snow filled the trench paths. It was so white it was like being in the darkest dark. When people walked outside they became confused. They would be turned around by the wind and would soon lose their way. Although the village was small, the parents were afraid their children would become lost on the way home from school and that they might even freeze to death before they could be found.

Mrs. Elliott was the teacher in the one-room schoolhouse. When the blizzard trapped the children inside, she gathered them around her. Dressed in their outdoor clothes the students sat close together on the wooden schoolroom floor and sang. Some songs they sang were in German and some in English. They waited for release from the storm.

Fighting the wind, the fathers tied one end of a rope to the school door and the other end to the nearest building, the huge communal dining hall and kitchen where the mothers had gathered.

After the rope was securely tied, the men and women groped their way along the rope towards the schoolhouse to help their children. The men carried the smallest children and the women guided the older ones along the rope.

The blizzard wore itself out in three days, leaving in its wake gray clouds, heavy and cold. The children bundled up, left their warm homes and ran to school. The biting winds stung and nipped their noses as they scrambled through the snowdrifts. In class they learned how to spell new words. They turned the pages of their arithmetic books and tried to do the problems that became more and more difficult.

The big children read to the little children who were still learning their ABC's. When they looked up from their work there was nothing to see outside because the snow was piled high against the windows.

And one day the sun came out. A chinook, a warm wind, blew in from across the Rocky Mountains. The children opened the door and crowded against the windows to look in wonder at the new and shining white world.

Bustling with happiness, they begged, "Will you take us for a walk, Mrs. Elliott?"

"Oh, yes, let's go for a walk," she answered. "Let's go for a walk in the beautiful new white world."

They trudged across the fields. Soon they noticed that they were not the only ones exploring and enjoying the sun, the soft warm winds and the boundless expanse of fresh snow.

"Who has left footprints in the snow?" they asked.

"Who do you think leaves tracks like that?" replied Mrs. Elliott.

"We know!" shouted the children. "We know and we see him. He has taken off his brown summer coat and put on his white one to match the snow."

They found more tracks. "Who ran by here?" they asked. "Who ran by here and over the hills, Mrs. Elliott?"

In the distance they could see a blur of movement but it was so far away that they could not make it out. They followed the tracks across the field, through the woods, over the frozen pond and up the far-off hill.

As they came close they saw it was a coyote. His front paw was held fast in a terrible iron trap which was chained to a stake driven into the snow. Feathers were scattered on the circular path the animal had trodden around the stake. The coyote had been hoodwinked. Trappers had left a dead chicken in the trap, hoping to entice an animal starving after the days he had lain hidden from the storm.

"Help him!" cried the children.

"Stay here," whispered Mrs. Elliott. The children drew close to one another, all except one boy who stood very still, his arms clasped tightly around his body and his face almost buried in his scarf.

Mrs. Elliott dropped to her knees and slowly crept toward the coyote. She talked softly to him. "Don't be afraid. Don't be afraid. I will not hurt you. I shall try to help you. Don't be afraid." The coyote pulled away as far as he could.

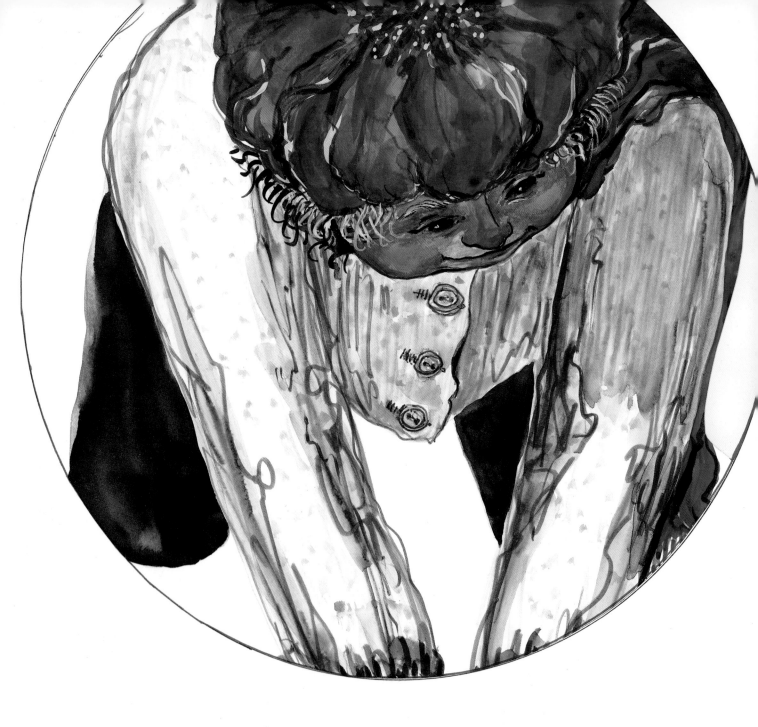

She talked softly to him. With all the strength she had she pressed open the jaws of the trap. The coyote stared into Mrs. Elliott's face but he did not remove his paw from the trap.

"You must take your paw out of the trap," said Mrs. Elliott quietly. "You must take it out right now because I cannot hold the trap open much longer." The coyote did not move. Gently Mrs. Elliott spoke to him again. "You must cooperate. You must take your paw out of the trap." The coyote pulled back his paw.

He backed away a step and sat holding his paw up as if it hurt. After a moment he gingerly tested the paw. He bowed low to Mrs. Elliott and then he stood up, threw back his head and howled.

"Run," screamed the children. "Run before the trappers come back. You are free."

But the coyote did not run. He stood, wagging his tail, watching the children and Mrs. Elliott. His fur, ruffled by the breeze, sparkled in the sunlight. Mrs. Elliott got to her feet and joined the children. She put her arms around the boy who had kept apart.

"He is fine," she said. "He is free."

The children and Mrs. Elliott walked backwards, watching the coyote. He did not move. Everyone stopped. The children looked at Mrs. Elliott and then they looked at the coyote. Mrs. Elliott called softly to him one more time. "You are free. Run fast." The coyote cocked his ears and wagged his tail.

He threw back his head and howled once more. The sound echoed back from the wood and the hills. He turned and trotted a few feet away. He spun around and looked again at Mrs. Elliott and the children.

He ran to the top of the next knoll. Again he faced them. From his throat came a wavering, haunting call that reached to the sky, that wound and drifted through the forest. He cast one last look over his shoulder and disappeared over the crest of the hill.

No one talked. Even the smallest child was somber and thoughtful as they retraced their path back to the school. As they neared their destination a weary little girl asked the question all the other children were thinking of asking.

"Why didn't he bite, Mrs. Elliott?"
She answered, "He knew we loved him."